For Florence
and all of those who make their voices heard.
— *J. F. D.*

THE SHEEP GO ON STRIKE

Written and illustrated by

JEAN-FRANÇOIS DUMONT

Eerdmans Books for Young Readers

Grand Rapids, Michigan • Cambridge, U.K.

One day on the farm, there was a revolution.
Everyone knew about it.
The sheep were on strike!

It was Ernest who came up with the idea. He climbed up on a trough and began to speak: "Why are we always the ones who get sheared? Why don't they make cat-hair sweaters, duck-down socks, or donkey-hair britches?" Everyone in the flock was listening and nodding.

Encouraged, Ernest continued with even more conviction: "And who is cold come October, when the meadow is covered with ice every morning?"

The sheep looked at each other.

The boldest one replied: "Uh . . . we are?"

"Who is it that starts to cough and sneeze because of that?"

"We do!"

"And who has to swallow disgusting medicine and get shots from the vet to get well?"

"WE DO!"

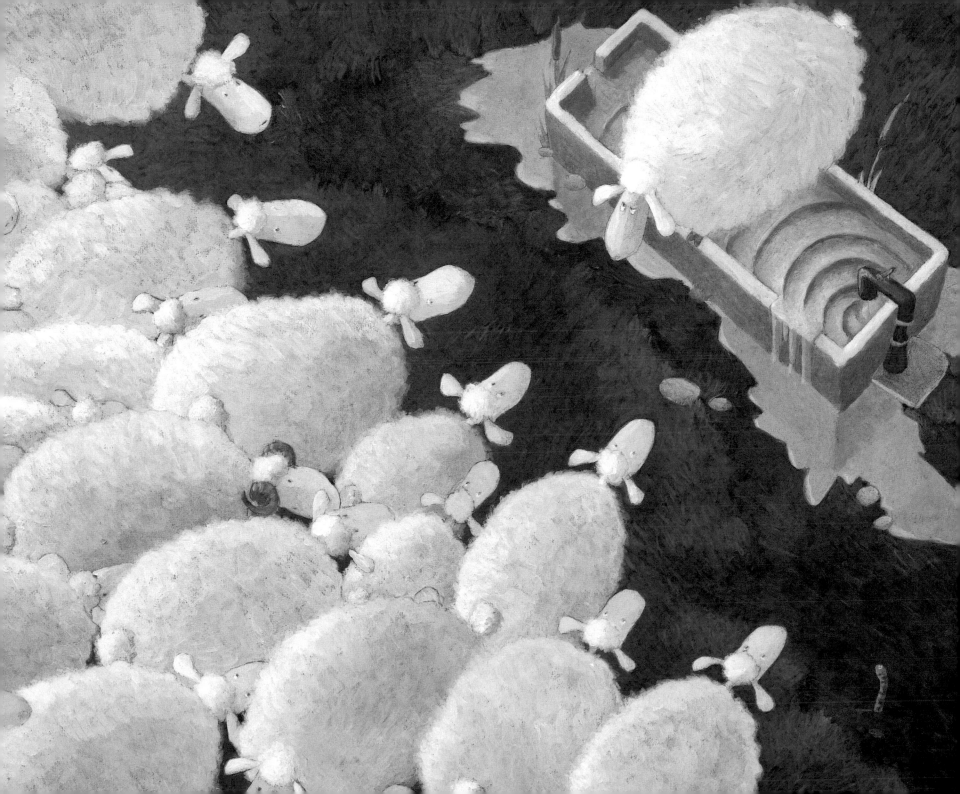

"All that — for what?
Just to graze on short grass and drink icy water!"

"It's true!" the sheep shouted.

"But we're done with that! We won't be afraid!
Let's refuse to be sheared!
Everyone who agrees, raise your hoof!"

They all raised their hooves, down to the last sheep.
And that's how the strike began.

After that day, the sheep camped out in their meadow,
refusing to move.
Ralph, the sheepdog, didn't know what to make of it.

At first, he tried to get the sheep to obey him by nipping one of the ewes — but the flock nearly stampeded him, running after him and hollering about police brutality! After that, he stayed in his doghouse and refused to talk with delegates from the flock.

On the farm, the opinions were divided. Some, like Igor the goose, thought that sheep were made to be shorn. That was the tradition; that was how it was supposed to be. Zita, the littlest goose, was more understanding. "They must be freezing without their thick wool," she said. "They must be awfully hot and then terribly cold."

Mr. Brown frowned. "I don't think I could stand all that hair on my back — it must itch."

"Oh, not at all, my dear sir!" Edgar the rat interjected. "On the contrary, it's very comfortable. And very warm!"

With a lot of brouhaha, everyone joined in the conversation, giving their opinions on the comfort of the sheep's wool. Fortunately, night eventually fell, and the farm became quiet again.

The next day, a big march was planned on the road that ran from the end of the meadow to the goose pond. The sheep organized to create slogans and establish the marching order. The others watched the preparations. Some of the little chicks had planned to join the procession as a sign of support, but the rooster threatened to send them back to the chicken coop. The hens cackled: "This is not going to end well; this business is not going to end well at all . . ."

The dogs from the neighboring farms, alerted by Ralph, gathered around the doghouse.
"These sheep have gone mad. They nearly ran me over! If the other flocks hear about this, we may have a general strike on our hands, and then . . ."

A rust-colored dog lowered his ears, let out a little yap, and added: "Then we'll all lose our jobs . . ."

Meanwhile, the march had begun.
The rams started things off.
They unrolled a big banner and began to chant:
"Sheep, yes! Meek doves, no!"
The rest of the flock joined in the refrain:
"Sheep, yes! Meek doves, no!"

Of course, in the farm's dovecote, this slogan
wasn't exactly appreciated, and the doves
flocked to boo the demonstrators.

The sheep ignored the shouts and continued with even more resolve.
Some of the other animals joined their cause and marched with them.
Others took the side of the doves, and insults were thrown back and forth.
The procession, now almost running, rounded the henhouse and . . .
there were the dogs, determined to make everyone return to the sheep pen!

The next day, the farm was in chaos.
While the chickens counted the feathers
they had lost in the scuffle, the hens cackled:
"We knew that this wouldn't turn out well!"

As they tended to their bumps and bruises, the animals didn't feel very proud of themselves. Never in anyone's memory had there ever been a brawl on the farm!

Zita thought out loud: "There must be some way to make the sheep happy."

"But without the sheep's wool," the donkey brayed, "the farm would go bankrupt!"

A fat black hen shook her comb: "After all, we give our eggs every morning."

"Not all of them, luckily, not all of them!" a little chick shouted at the top of his voice.

Rosalie jumped: "That's it, that's the solution!"

Curious, the animals gathered around her, and the little pig explained her idea. "With some of the wool, maybe we could . . . "

Shearing day arrived — and, strangely, the sheep didn't look all that unhappy. Under Ralph's watchful eye, they went in turn into the sheep pen and came out a few minutes later without their thick layers of wool. Soon, everyone in the flock had been sheared.

At nightfall, there was an unusual buzz of activity on the farm. Everyone was busy; one after the other they came and went, and strange clicking sounds came from the henhouse, the hutches, and the stable.

Early the next morning, the rooster, worn out by his sleepless night, still found the strength to crow. The sun came up, and everyone finally discovered the sheep's stylish new outfits . . .

Published in 2014 by Eerdmans Books for Young Readers,
an imprint of Wm. B. Eerdmans Publishing Co.
2140 Oak Industrial Dr. NE
Grand Rapids, Michigan 49505
P.O. Box 163, Cambridge CB3 9PU U.K.

www.eerdmans.com/youngreaders

Manufactured at Tien Wah Press
in Malaysia in April 2014, first printing

19 18 17 16 15 14   9 8 7 6 5 4 3 2 1

Library of Congress Cataloging-in-Publication Data

Dumont, Jean-François, 1959- author, illustrator.
[Grève des moutons. English]
The sheep go on strike / by Jean-François Dumont ; illustrated by
Jean-François Dumont ; [translated by Leslie Mathews].
pages cm
Summary: When the sheep on a farm go on strike rather than having
their warm coats sheared off, the other animals begin taking sides
until, at last, a compromise can be reached.
ISBN 978-0-8028-5470-4
[1. Strikes and lockouts — Fiction. 2. Sheep — Fiction. 3. Domestic
animals — Fiction. 4. Farm life — Fiction.]
I. Mathews, Leslie. II. Title.
PZ7.D89367She 2014
[E] — dc23
2013044350

ILLUSTRATOR ON STRIKE

NO IMAGES ON THESE PAGES